Un

SEA

An imprint of Om Books International

 **Om Books International**

Reprinted in 2021

Corporate & Editorial Office
A-12, Sector 64, Noida 201 301
Uttar Pradesh, India
Phone: +91 120 477 4100
Email: editorial@ombooks.com
Website: www.ombooksinternational.com

Sales Office
107, Ansari Road, Darya Ganj
New Delhi 110 002, India
Phone: +91 11 4000 9000
Email: sales@ombooks.com
Website: www.ombooks.com

© Om Books International 2017

ISBN: 978-93-86108-20-3

Printed in India

10 9 8 7 6 5 4 3 2

Under the
SEA

Paste your
photograph here

My name is

_____

May was on a fishing trip with **her dad**.

May loved **the sea. She** loved **the** fresh **air and the** cool, blue water. **She** could **not** wait to catch a fish.

May's **dad** showed **her the** fishing **rod**.

It **had** a string at **one end**. At **the end** of **the** string, there **was** a hook.

Then, **May's dad** opened a small **box**.

"**Eew!**" said **May**. **The box was** full of worms!

"This is bait, **May**," said **Dad**. "We will catch fish with **the** help of these worms."

"**Yuk!**" said **May**.

Once **the** fishing **rod was** ready, **May**'s **dad** threw **the** hook into **the** water.

"**Now** what?" asked **May**.

"**Now**, we wait," said **Dad**, smiling at **May**.

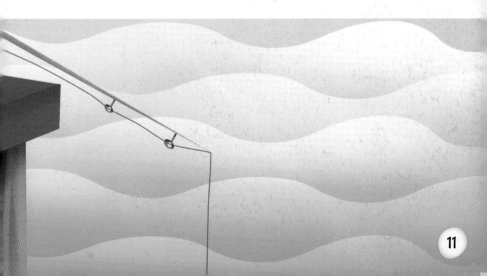

"Ugh!" said **May**. **She did not** like waiting.

Every **two** minutes, **May** checked **the box** of **ice**.

But it **had** nothing just **yet**.

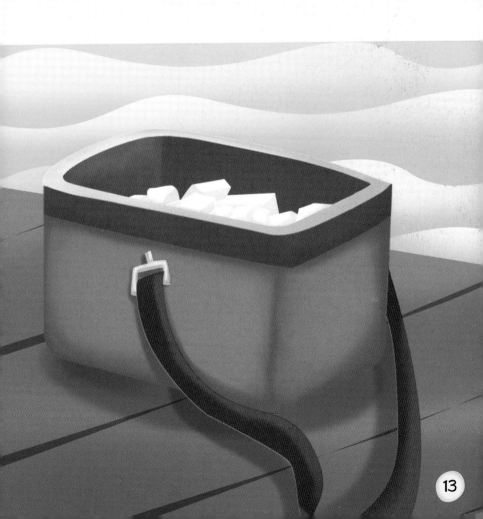

Finally, **May sat** closer to **the** water.

There were **wee** little fish in it.
May fed them bread crumbs.

How she wished **she** could
swim in **the sea** with them!

All of a sudden, **May** lost **her** balance **and she** fell.

May saw that **she was** under water!

"**Are you** lost?" **She** heard a voice **ask her**.

May turned around. It **was** a tiny **eel**!

"I'm **not** lost," said **May**, "I think I fell in."

"Oh!" said **the eel** stretching **out** a **fin**, "I am **Eve the eel**."

May was about to shake hands when a **cod** fish **cut** in.

"**Eve, Eve you** have to come **and** help! **Gus the** guppy is trapped in a **net!**"

Eve and the cod fish rushed **off**. **May** followed.

They went to an **old ark. Gus was** stuck in a **net.**

Both **Eve and the cod** fish tried to **cut the net, but** could **not.**

"I **may** be able to help," said **May.**

23

May tried to untie **the net**.
But the knot **was too** tight.
So, **May** used **her** strong teeth.
With a **nip and** a **cut**, **the net**
fell away. **Gus was set** free!

Eve, **Gus and the cod** fish thanked **May**.

"I'm Cody," said **the cod** fish, "Thank **you for** saving **Gus**."

May was about to reply. **But** a **big** hook caught **her** by **her** shirt.

It yanked **her out** of **the** water.

May woke up. **She was** still on **the** pier! It **was all** a dream!

"No fish today," said **her dad**. **The box** of **ice was** empty.

"That's great," said **May** smiling, "They **are** better **off** under **the sea**."

Count the number of worms in the box. Write the correct number under the box.

Draw a line from the fish to its shadow.

Colour the bubbles of the things that are found underwater.

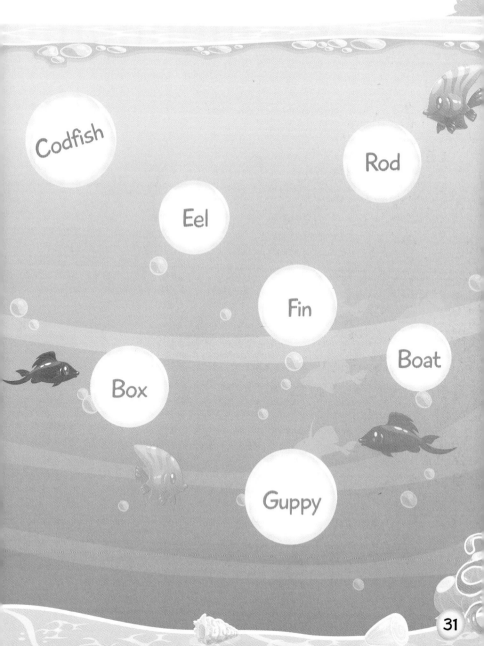

Codfish

Rod

Eel

Fin

Boat

Box

Guppy

Know your words

Sight Words

was	now	off	and
the	two	old	did
not	yet	but	wee
had	how	nip	are
one	you	big	too
end	she	out	for
yuk	her	all	

Naming Words

May	box	Gus	dad
sea	eel	cod	eve
air	fin	ark	
rod	net	ice	

Doing Words

sat	saw	cut	set
fed	ask		